BRITISH TERRITORY

...an

...Villages

...ton Sioux

Mississippi R.

...t Mound

"Meeting" Yankton Sioux

Missouri R.

St. Charles

St. Louis

UNITED STATES

• Pittsburgh

Ohio

Washington D.C. ★

ATLANTIC OCEAN

THE EXPEDITION'S

ROUTE

WEST

1803-1805

GULF of MEXICO

Seaman's Journal
On the Trail with Lewis and Clark

Our appreciation and thanks go to Dorothy Twohig, Editor-in-Chief Emeritus, The Papers of George Washington, University of Virginia, for reading this manuscript and offering her comments and help.

Seaman's Journal
On the Trail with Lewis and Clark

BY PATRICIA REEDER EUBANK

ideals children's books™

Nashville, Tennessee

ISBN 0-8249-5442-4

Published by Ideals Children's Books, an imprint of
Ideals Publications, a division of Guideposts
535 Metroplex Drive, Suite 250
Nashville, Tennessee 37211
www.idealsbooks.com

Color separations by Precision Color Graphics,
Franklin, Wisconsin

Printed and bound in Mexico by R. R. Donnelley.

10 9 8 7 6 5 4 3

Library of Congress Cataloging-in-Publication Data

Eubank, Pattricia Reeder.
    Seaman's journal : on the trail with Lewis and Clark
/ written and illustrated by Patricia Reeder Eubank.
    p. cm.
Summary: Seaman, the Newfoundland dog belonging
to Meriwether Lewis, keeps an account of their
adventures during the journey to the Pacific.
    ISBN 0-8249-5442-4 (alk. paper)
1. Lewis and Clark Expedition (1804-1806)--Juvenile
fiction. 2. Seaman (Dog)--Juvenile fiction. [1. Lewis
and Clark Expedition (1803-1806)--Fiction. 2 Seaman
(Dog)--Fiction. 3. Dogs--Fiction. 4. Newfoundland
dog--Fiction.] 1. Title.
    PZ7.E864 Se 2002
[Fic]--dc21

For my husband,

A true mountain man and

adventurer.

With all my love,

P. R. E.

A Word from Seaman

My name is Seaman. I am a male dog from Pennsylvania, and Meriwether Lewis paid twenty dollars for me. I am a Newfoundland. I have two coats of fur, a thick soft undercoat and a long silky outer coat so I never get cold. I love water and have big, furry, webbed feet, which make me an excellent swimmer. I weigh almost 150 pounds. We Newfoundlands love children and are very loyal. I will protect my master with my life. Here is my story of the greatest adventure a dog ever had when I followed Lewis and Clark all the way to the Pacific Ocean and back again.

ME AT 2 MONTHS

PITTSBURGH, PENNSYLVANIA, AUGUST 1803

I have a new master, Captain Meriwether Lewis. We are in Pittsburgh waiting for our keelboat to be built.

President Jefferson chose Lewis to be in charge of an expedition called the Corps of Discovery. We are to find a route to the Pacific Ocean. I am in charge of Lewis.

KEELBOAT

FORT WOOD, MISSOURI, APRIL 1804

Lewis and I have been here for the past nine months. I've
hauled barrels of flour, cornmeal, sugar, salt, coffee, apples, and
hard biscuits. Lewis has studied maps and books about fossils,
plants, and medicine. We've packed shiny bracelets, scissors,
medals, mirrors, army uniforms, hats, and flags to trade with the
Indians. Sometimes Lewis and I study the stars all night.

SUGAR

LEWIS'S AIR GUN

Saint Charles, Missouri, May 14, 1804

Lewis, along with his best friend and co-leader William Clark, thirty-one men, and I are off! In a pouring rain, we pushed the fifty-five-foot keelboat and two pirogues (flat-bottomed dugout canoes), into the Missouri River. We travel upriver and the men must push against its strong current.

Camp along the Missouri River, May 22, 1804

A party of Kickapoos came into our camp. We gave them trinkets. They gave us deer meat. The men were so hungry there was almost nothing left for me!

WILLIAM CLARK

KICKAPOO

ALONG THE MISSOURI RIVER, MAY 23, 1804

Most days Lewis and I walk along the riverbank as Clark steers the keelboat. Often, huge flocks of passenger pigeons block out the sun. Lewis sketches them in his journal while I look out for rattlesnakes.

While I was splashing in the muddy river, chasing after fish, Lewis fell off a limestone cliff! Luckily, he caught himself on a ledge and was saved. From now on, I'll keep my eye on Captain Lewis.

AT THE KANSAS AND PLATTE RIVERS, JUNE–JULY 1804

There are many beavers here. There are also some nasty-tempered badgers. I love to pounce at the prairie dogs, or "barking squirrels," as they pop their heads out of the ground. My favorite animal to chase is the squirrel. When I catch one, I take him to Cook. He is glad to get it.

MISSOURI RIVER, NORTH OF PLATTE RIVER, AUGUST 1804

The Oto and Missouri Indians invited Lewis and Clark to a Council meeting where I helped Clark pass out coats, blankets, flags, and medals. Lewis spoke of peace and explained that the French and Spanish had sold the land to a "new Great Father," the president of the United States. Mornings are cooler now and the geese are flying south. Today we saw our first coyote, or prairie wolf.

BUFFALO

Big Sioux River, August 25, 1804

We heard an Indian legend about the Spirit Mound. The legend says men only eighteen inches tall with huge heads live at the mound. Lewis, the men, and I started across the prairie. It was so hot that Lewis sent me back, but the men walked for three hours before reaching the mound. They saw no men, but buffalo covered the prairie. I spent the afternoon lying in the cool riverbank. A hot, dry prairie is no place for a Newfoundland.

ON THE PLAINS OF THE DAKOTA, SEPTEMBER 1804

I trail Lewis up steep hills and down deep valleys. We've seen bobcat, elk, buffalo, and antelope. I chased the antelope and took one to Cook. One day we counted thirty-six bald eagles soaring above our heads!

SIOUX

TOBACCO BAG

Off Teton River, September 1804

We named this river Teton River, but the Teton Sioux call it "Bad River." The only thing bad are the manners of the Sioux! They carried my master on a painted buffalo robe to their camp. They placed him on a white buffalo skin where he smoked the peace pipe with the council chiefs. When we started toward our boat to leave, the Sioux grabbed the boat's rope to stop us. They wanted tobacco and our pirogue. When Lewis threw tobacco at the chief, they let us go.

I was glad to get away. The Sioux eat dogs!

PIPE

TOMAHAWK

VILLAGE OF THE ARIKARAS, OCTOBER 9, 1804

The Arikaras are farmers and shared beans, corn, and squash with us. The men were glad for the vegetables, but this is not food for Seaman!

The Arikaras children played games with Clark's servant, York. He pretended he was a lion and roared at them. They pretended they were scared and ran away. I pretended I was on guard and barked! What fun we had!

ARIKARA

FORT MANDAN, NOVEMBER 1804

It is very cold. My fur keeps me warm, but the men suffer. We have met the
Mandan and the Hidatsa tribes. Both are peaceful farmers. The men have built a
camp and named it in honor of the Mandans.

A French Canadian fur trader named Toussaint Charbonneau came into
camp, and Lewis hired him as interpreter and cook. His Shoshone wife,
Sacajawea, is about fourteen. Her name means "Bird Girl."

Charbonneau is a good cook and shares his meat
with me!

FORT MANDAN, DECEMBER 25, 1804

We had a Christmas party. The men played tambourines, fiddles, and trumpets. Even the Mandans danced. We all had a great time.

JANUARY–FEBRUARY 1805

The snow is very deep. The men hunt deer and rabbit for food, and they hollow out trunks of cottonwood trees and make canoes. Often Lewis and I visit the Mandans and Hidatsas who live close by. They tell him about the route over the mountains, and Lewis writes it all down in his journal.

WHORTLEBERRY

FORT MANDAN, FEBRUARY 11, 1805

I help Sacajawea dig roots to eat. She also gathers plants for medicine. One day she made *pemmican* and gave me a piece. I ate the dried meat in it but spit out the nuts and berries. Phooey!

Sacajawea is a mom now and I have a baby to watch over. She named her baby Jean Baptiste Charbonneau. Clark calls him "Pompey," or "Pomp." Will he call me "Uncle Seaman?"

EVERGREEN HUCKLEBERRY

PEMMICAN HAMMER

ROOTS

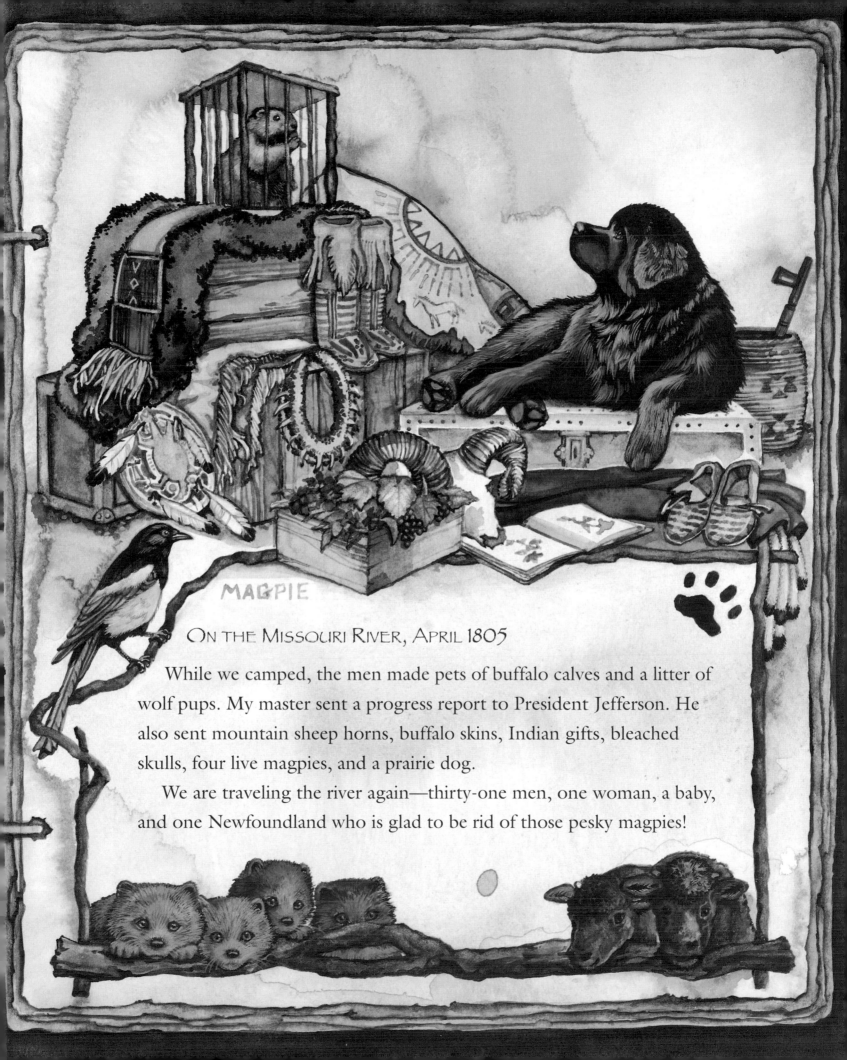

MAGPIE

ON THE MISSOURI RIVER, APRIL 1805

While we camped, the men made pets of buffalo calves and a litter of
wolf pups. My master sent a progress report to President Jefferson. He
also sent mountain sheep horns, buffalo skins, Indian gifts, bleached
skulls, four live magpies, and a prairie dog.

We are traveling the river again—thirty-one men, one woman, a baby,
and one Newfoundland who is glad to be rid of those pesky magpies!

AT THE MOUTH OF
THE YELLOWSTONE RIVER,
APRIL–MAY 1805

So many buffalo, antelope, and elk roam here. One day, two grizzly bears attacked us. Lewis shot and wounded one. He ran away but the other chased us until Lewis shot him. The grizzly's paws were eleven inches wide with seven-inch claws.

Then a mean old beaver bit my leg. I bled so much that Lewis thought I would die, but my master saved me. I can't die. I have an expedition to guard!

CAMP ON THE MISSOURI RIVER, MAY 14, 1805

Sacajawea is a hero! Lewis and I were walking along the water's edge while the rest of the men were in the canoes and pirogues. The wind came up, the sky turned black, lightning flashed, thunder roared, and the river began to churn. Charbonneau was in the lead boat with most of our supplies, but he lost control and the gear went overboard. Sacajawea held Pomp with one hand while, with her other, she scooped out all that she could reach. My master is heartbroken; his journal was lost. But my journal did not even get damp!

MAY 29, 1805

I am a hero too! Last night while all the men were asleep, I heard a noise. Suddenly a gigantic buffalo charged into camp, straight for Lewis's tent! I barked out, "Woof!" That buffalo turned around and headed back to where he came from. Lewis called me his brave dog!

LEWIS' WOODPECKER

SALMON BERRY

AT THE SOURCE OF THE MISSOURI RIVER, AUGUST 1805

As Lewis and I walked near the river we named for President Jefferson, we found the source of the Missouri River. We drank from the small trickle of icy water that bubbled out of the ground. Now we know there will be no river route all the way to the Pacific Ocean. We will have to walk or ride horses over the Bitterroot Mountains, which we named for a bitter-tasting plant.

LEMHI RIVER, AUGUST 1805

Sacajawea told us how the Hidatsas had kidnapped her from the Shoshones when she was just a little girl. When we met up with a party of Shoshones, Lewis and Clark bought thirty horses from them. When we were led to Shoshone Chief Cameahwait, Sacajawea recognized him as her brother! Sacajawea cried with joy. And I cried too.

LEWIS' MONKEYFLOWER

Bitterroot Mountains, October 9, 1805

Our guide, a Shoshone named Old Toby, has guided us in the mountains. But he has suddenly left us, and we wandered around lost for a whole day. During the past two months, we have walked through rain, sleet, and snowstorms. We met the Flatheads and traded for fresh horses. The men do not find game and we are hungry for fresh meat. We drink melted snow and eat candles. We are even glad to have the soup that Lewis made and dried in St. Louis.

FLATHEAD

CANDLE MOLD

THE COLUMBIA RIVER, OCTOBER 6, 1805

When we reached the western edge of the mountains, we met the Nez Percé, who have pierced noses and are friendly. They guided us, and Lewis left horses for our return trip with them. Now the snow has turned to rain and there is fog day and night. The men portage around the river's rapids.

PACIFIC OCEAN, NOVEMBER 7, 1805

Last night we camped on a hill. This morning I heard the shout, "Ocean in view!" Imagine, a dog from Pennsylvania standing at the Pacific Ocean! We are all happy.

NEZ PERCE

CAMAS LILY

FORT CLATSOP

WHISTLING SWAN

OTTERS

SALMON

FORT CLATSOP, DECEMBER 1805

The men have built a fort from the pine and fir trees. It rains constantly now, and many of the men wear the Clatsops' basket hats to keep their heads dry. We live on fish and whale blubber from the Chinooks. Clark works to complete his maps while Lewis studies the animals, especially the sea otter. Clark said we have come 4,142 miles from Missouri to the Pacific!

CLATSOP HAT

LAZY SEAMAN

COLUMBIA RIVER, MARCH 23, 1806

We are back on the river and heading home!

APRIL 1806

I was kidnapped by the Chinook, but my wonderful master sent three men to rescue me. He told them to shoot if necessary to get me back. But they let me go. I am glad to be back guarding my master.

WALLA WALLA

SAGE GROUSE

BITTERROOT MOUNTAINS, MAY 1806

The snow in the mountains is still deep and we had to turn back. For several days, we stayed with the friendly Walla Wallas, then we found the Nez Percé. They welcomed us, fed us, and returned the horses that we had left with them. They will guide us through the mountains as they did when we first crossed this land.

SWIFT FOX

MISSOURI RIVER, AUGUST 12, 1806

Lewis and Clark split our corps into two parties to explore the Louisiana Purchase Territory. It was hard for both groups. Lewis was hurt and Clark's horses were stolen. We were glad when we were reunited.

At the end of June, we said goodbye to the Bitterroot Mountains. We also said goodbye to Charbonneau and Sacajawea. Now, Lewis and I walk the riverbank as usual, but I miss Sacajawea and little Pomp.

SALAL

OWL'S CLOVER

SAINT CHARLES, MISSOURI, SEPTEMBER 21, 1806

The whole town turned out to greet us. They thought we had died in the wilderness. We did not die. We have been on the greatest adventure ever. Lewis will send a long report to President Jefferson about the Indian tribes, plants, and animals we discovered. Clark has mapped the lands we crossed.

And I, Seaman, have brought my wise, brave, and dedicated master safely home.

Sacajawea's Pemmican

Place 1 cup of broken beef or buffalo jerky, 1 cup dried cranberries, and 1 cup nuts or sunflower seeds in a blender; grind until well mixed. Set aside. In a microwave-safe bowl, combine 2 teaspoons honey and ¼ cup peanut butter. Microwave 20 seconds or just until peanut butter is softened. Stir meat and nut mixture into peanut butter mixture. Press mixture into a plastic-lined 8 x 8-inch baking dish. Cut into bars. Cover tightly and store in refrigerator.

Fort Clatsop

Lewis's Route

Clearwater R.

Columbia R.

Lochsa R.

Great Falls Missouri R.

Clark's Route

Reunion
For

Salmon R.

Three Falls

Yellowstone R.

Knife R.

OREGON
TERRITORY

Lemhi Pass

Gallitin R.

Madison R.

Jefferson R.

Snake R.

Missouri

SPANISH
TERRITORY

Rocky Mtns

Platte

Kansas

LOUISIA
PURCHA

THE

EXPEDITION'S

RETURN ROUTE

PACIFIC
OCEAN